FORBIDDEN LOVE

A SINGLE DAD NANNY ROMANCE

SAVANNAH KOLE

Forbidden Love
Copyright © 2026 by Savannah Kole
All rights reserved.

Book Cover and formatting provided by Trisha Fuentes
https://linktr.ee/trishafuentes

↳ <u>ABOUT US</u>

Ardent Artist Books was established in 2008. We publish modern and historical romances several times a month!

Get Your FREE Download:
Published & Upcoming Books
Visit our website at:
https://bit.ly/3Wva4o0

↳ <u>WATCH THE BOOK TRAILER</u>

Follow us on YouTube!
https://www.youtube.com/@theardentartist

Like, Subscribe & Comment

CONTENTS

ONE

A MAN DROVE his family off his compound towards the big city where he and his wife worked. His house was just a kilometer away from the big city, but traffic made it seem like a four-hour drive. He worked at one of those prestigious hospitals in the city. He had to drop his daughter off to school first before proceeding to their work place. His wife and child were having fun singing their favorite song off the top of their voices. They did this often to lessen the boredom brought on by the long traffic hours. He smiled in pure bliss before joining in with his bass voice. These were the moments he enjoyed the most, with the traffic congestion somehow like a blessing in disguise. He had time to spend with them before the long hours at work. Singing with them in the car in the morning was a pleasant way to start the day, and he couldn't ask for anything better than that. Seeing his wife and child this happy was a joy on its own.

His name was Dr. Dante Russo: a handsome, medium height, well-built, thirty-four-year-old. His wife was Beth: also a doctor, and a beautiful, slim, light-skinned thirty-two-year-old, and their precious little daughter Skylar, was an adorable, curious five-year-old. Her parents and friends fondly called her '*Sky*'.

Dante and Beth both worked at Masters Orthopedic Medical Centre. They had met back in college where they both studied the same course. Their relationship had started off in a weird way. The two of them being brilliant, often got into arguments about contents of one course or another. Over time they exchanged ideas, and how they understood the units in their different perspectives. And before they knew it, they had fallen in love with each other. They agreed to disagree in everything, and they never left a problem unresolved. They made an interesting couple in the beginning, and their close friends would just shake their heads at them. This did not deter them. They were determined to make it work and they used what they learned in their studies on themselves. Selflessness, kindness, patience, love and most of all, understanding. At the end of their studies, they had resolved to get married and live together after graduating. And a year later Skylar was born. She was an angel, a lovely child.

Luck seemed to have followed them since they both found residency in the same hospital. Masters Orthopedic was one of the best clinics, and so they began their successful careers. They were kind, caring, thoughtful and loving and they fit perfectly well within the orthopedic practice which demanded people with a high level of understanding and composure to deal with the patients that came to see them. Dealing with people of all kinds of bone breaks was not everyone's cup of tea. But these two, knew their way around it.

They were both at their early thirties but they had won many people's hearts. They were what they termed as 'perfect or power couple' in the community. Many times people had sought advice from them concerning marital issues, and they were always ready to help, thus saving many marriages from falling apart. They were always concerned and this brought joy and harmony in their house.

In the evening of every other day for them, they would sit down and discuss the events of the day over a cup of hot chocolate. They unburdened their fears and experiences to each other which helped them to relax and feel lighter. They were each other's best friends. When they retired to bed, they slept peacefully.

Besides being medical practitioners, they were fun lovers too. They could go out hiking and camping while hunting on weekend getaways with their golden retriever, Taylor. On such days, Sky would stay back with Marni Hill, her nanny.

Nanny Marni, as Sky would call her, would play with her for the whole time her parents were away. Marni was twenty-six, and she adored this little girl. She would tell her lots of stories and read her fairy tale books. Sky had turned out to be a very brilliant child as she learnt a lot in such a short time. At her young age she had mastered the human anatomy, a field that older kids were struggling to learn. Sky and Marni were so close, Sky preferred her nanny's company compared to her mother because she put everything else on hold to always help her first whenever she needed help. She also allowed her to help in the house whenever she folded her washed clothes. She was learning how to be responsible at such a tender age. Other kids would be playing games on PlayStation during their free time, but not Skylar.

DANTE AND BETH had several things in common too, they shared a birth date—the ninth of September. Every year, the clinic had made it an exceptional day for them to be out to celebrate their day however they wanted. Each year their love for fun made it more interesting trying out new things and going to new places.

During work hours though, they could not sit in the office for long. They would do their rounds in the hospital, visit their patients and helped the caretakers on how to deal with each patient's ailments. Most of their patients were kids and they cared about them as much as they cared about Skylar. They believed that the kids were special in a way and those who had a permanent disability could still discover their talents and life would be much better for everyone. They believed that disability was never an inability. It was in this spirit that they had improved the facilities in the hospital. Providing their patients with a very comfortable environment while they recuperated in that hospital. To them it was important to discover a child's ability to do something at a younger age. That way, it was easy to make their lives a little bit tolerable and more so worth living.

TWO

THE WEEKEND WAS FAST APPROACHING and the couple had plans as usual. They travelled once a month, mostly at the end when work was not packed, and they had saved enough to travel, although money for them was never a problem.

They wanted to visit the famous *Crystal Waters,* in the tropical islands of Maldives. They had heard so much about these waters, and were willing to explore it during a vacation for just the two of them. Many would think that they were forgetting little Skylar, but they preferred she'd be safe in the hands of the nanny at home. But they always made sure to bring her gifts to make up for their absence and the little girl was delighted whenever she received presents too. It could be a nice dress, spoons for her collection, bracelets, shoes and many more, and she stored the jewelry in a little box under her bed. Her parents would then tell her stories about where they had visited and promised to take her when she grew up.

Crystal Waters was a beach on a tropic island. They did an early booking on Friday evening for a certain hotel room close to the beach so that they could have as much fun in the water without worrying about where they would sleep. They had gotten used to such plans since they travelled a lot.

Beth asked Marni to pack their bags for the trip, and Marni got to it immediately even though she knew her boss was going to recheck whatever she had packed. Marni never questioned Beth, she made sure the swimsuits were packed as it was quite obvious that they were going to swim. By sundown on Friday, two bags were already packed and waiting for the trip. Marni wished they could take her to such trips too, but then she remembered that her job was to be a nanny and Skylar was right there with her.

Maybe someday they would travel together, she thought silently.

When Saturday morning came, all was set. The couple being early risers plus the excitement of reaching the beach when the sun was hot enough to warm the water, they bid their goodbyes to their daughter asking Marni to take good care of their little girl.

Nanny Marni took the opportunity as a big break for her and the little girl. She played with her, took her out for a walk, bought her favorite ice-cream and made sure she was happy such that she never missed her parents.

A plane ride and several hours later, the Russo's were finally at their destination. The island paradise was far more amazing than what they had pictured. The entrance to the resort was grand, the gate was huge, and well decorated with ornate carvings of dolphins huge enough to cover a group of tourists. The pavement was laced with floor tiles of red and white roses, daisies, violets as well as tulips. On the fences were tropical palms, ferns and jungle plants.

"Wow! This place is awesome," Beth exclaimed.

"It looks better than the internet pictures," Dante supported.

Two men came to welcome them and took their luggage to the reception while they admired the beautifully designed building they were going to spend their weekend in. A tropical oasis, the couple headed to the reception where their bags were already waiting.

"Hello," they greeted the receptionist.

"Welcome to the Crystal Waters Beach Hotel & Resort. How can I help you?" the friendly receptionist replied with a killer smile.

"Well, we're just checking in," Dante told her.

"Can I have your names so that I can check the bookings and room number assigned please?" she politely asked, as she looked at the computer waiting to enter the names of her clients.

"Dante and Beth Russo," he replied.

"I can see you booked a royal suite for five days. Here is your key. Those two gentlemen will take your luggage. And once again welcome to Crystal Waters Beach Hotel & Resort. I hope you will enjoy your stay," the receptionist replied again, with her simple but killer smile.

"Thanks miss, you can be sure we will enjoy our stay," Beth replied with excitement as they turned to follow the two gentlemen who were carrying their luggage.

THREE

ROOM EIGHT WAS right on the sand. A large room with lime green walls with amazing pieces of art hanging on every corner. The sitting area of the room were arranged with pieces of furniture, Navy blue octane seating Italian sofa sets surrounding flowery glass diamond-shaped tables. On the wall was a mounted large screen TV, a few meters beside it, was a fireplace, and above it lay a piece of painting of a peacock spreading its beautiful feathers. The dining area contained mahogany chairs and a large mahogany rectangular table. On top of the table was a fruit basket containing fresh apples.

The kitchen area was large with light blue kitchen cabinets and grey tiled walls. There were round seats across the counter. The place was exceptionally clean.

The fridge stood at the entrance. Moving to the bedroom, the Russo's jaw dropped in amazement. The walls were painted gray with a triangular yellow structure in the middle of every wall. In the middle of the room, lay a king-sized bed with white beddings and four white pillows. There were two computers set at a table on the furthest end of the room with two office chairs, and a reading lamp slightly above the computers. Slightly at the edge of the bed were two heart-shaped couches beige in color. The edges of the wall were strip lights. Beside the head of the bed were lamp stands in both sides. All the decorations were on point.

The most amazing part of the room for the Russo's was the view of the water through the glass window facing the beach. It felt like they were in a dreamland and they didn't want to wake up. It was so surreal.

"Honey, I think we're here for our second honeymoon," Dante said, holding his wife from behind.

"Perfect place to relax and enjoy this beautiful day. I think we should come here often and we should bring Sky along with us next time," Beth suggested.

"A great idea, I'm sure she would love the view. She really loves water. She always shouts when we pass through that fountain on our way to her school," agreed Dante.

"Speaking of water, I think we should change and head straight to the beach to kill our curiosity and to make sure our week doesn't just end before we have fun to our fullest," Beth said, grabbing her husband and dragging him to the closet where they changed to their swim gear.

A few minutes later they excitedly ran out of their room towards the beach leaving their key at the reception desk. The receptionist smiled at them—she knew this feeling—she had seen most of the couples who came to this place display the same kind of excitement. It was a happy place to create nice memories.

Dante and his wife held hands while racing in the terraces towards the beach like little kids.

The sun was just perfectly hot and the swim a welcome relief for most of the couples. Most of them were newlyweds on their honeymoon. The Russo's blended in just well, swimming and kayaking, and watching dolphins jump and dance in the water was pure bliss.

In the evening after having their dinner, they decided to go for a massage at the spa just within the hotel. It had been quite some time since they last went to any spa in the city, and so they were not taking another chance away from this. The masseuse, were doing a fantastic job and they felt so relaxed just ready for a night of sweet dreams and a bit of pleasure under the sheets.

The next morning, they woke up a little bit late as they had exhausted their energy the previous day. They called for room service breakfast: sandwiches, salads, sushi and a glass of fresh mango juice. They ate hungrily before they took a warm bath together in the bathtub. Taking turns to wash each other in the tub. Something that they have been doing each time they found themselves in the bathroom together. They knew each other's body like the palm of their hands.

ALL IS NOT what it appears to be.

What is revealed to be a happy, joyous couple could sometimes be deceiving, and the Russo's were no different. What you see on the surface does not always equal what is actually going on in the inside.

Life was mundane and boring sometimes, a routine that they both carved out for themselves. Sleep, work, eat, repeat, plus the occasional escape.

Arguments over moving out of state, selling their current house and purchasing a bigger one, resigning and setting up their own practices were a constant war of words, and reminders that they both worked too much, and little getaways like this were a necessity to regroup and recharge … even reconnect.

FOUR

TWO WEEKS LATER

THE GOVERNMENT HAD ANNOUNCED an outbreak of a killer disease called "COVID-19" which was caused by a coronavirus in the news, and warned people against going to public places or interacting with others who had travelled from certain countries. Most people didn't take the precaution seriously since they thought it was just a disease that didn't make sense. Shaking of hands and hugging were forms of greetings and it did not make sense stopping them just because the government said so.

It was a struggle to everyone since the impact had not been felt in California, and specifically, Los Angeles was not an exception. People still met, hugged and shook hands like nobody's business. Dante and Beth were no exceptions.

Since their hospital was known worldwide to provide the best orthopedic care, patients came from all over the world to get their treatment and assistance that their countries failed to provide. For that reason alone, the doctor's interacted with all who came across them. It was part of their job to be active and helpful.

"DARLING I WAS THINKING of going hiking this weekend. It's been so long since we took Taylor to some real trees," Beth suggested at one time to her husband. She had missed taking Taylor out to hunt in any woodland. She craved seeing Taylor run after wild rabbits or squirrels in the forest.

Dante and Beth were in the cafeteria at the clinic, discussing safe subjects so they wouldn't put on a display of discontented bliss.

"Sounds like a plan," Dante let go, jabbing his fork in his ranch-filled salad.

Beth merely pushed her fork around her caprese salad. "When should we go?"

Dante shrugged his shoulders and eyed other doctors sitting down for a lunch break. Then he rested his eyes on his wife. She had been pressing her fingers against her forehead for the past fifteen minutes. "What's wrong? Have a headache?"

Beth closed her eyes and lowered her eyes, "And a whopper of one."

"Did you take something?" He asked, careless now, not looking at her.

"Earlier," she whimpered, "But it hasn't seem to help."

Dante raised his eyes towards hers again, "Maybe you should lie down in the rest quarters for a few."

Beth shook her head, "Yeah, maybe. I've got so many patients I need to see today, I won't be able to take any time for myself."

Dante looked away for just a second—looked away at the new cute nurse who had just walked in—when he heard a thump, and the table shook unexpectedly. Whipping his head around, he scooted back his chair then went to reach for his wife who had passed out on the table.

"Beth!"

Hours later...

Dante rushed Beth to Cedars Sinai not knowing what to think of her sudden headache. Always believing the positive, he conjured up excuses of her being dehydrated, lack of sleep, stress, or even an ear infection.

Sighing heavily, Dante waited just outside the emergency room area. Eyeing doctors and nurses in protective gear rushing past him in a hurry. He had a bad feeling about what he saw, and slowly stood up on his feet.

Walking over to the examination room, he peered around the curtain to see the doctors and nurses who were examining his wife wear protective clothing.

"What the fuck is going on?!" He yelled at no one in particular.

No one was allowed to go into the area, not even a doctor like himself. No one was safe, no one was immune. He could only watch his wife from a safe distance. She was all sweaty and too weak to open her eyes. There were several tubes connected to her body.

A nurse who recognized him, came over to his side,

"Dr. Russo, we're doing everything we can. Why don't you have a seat?"

Dante was overwhelmed by fear of losing his wife—you don't realize what you have until it's gone. He walked up and down the hall, crossing his fingers that she actually would come out of there alive. She was the most important person in his life, together with his daughter.

There was a commotion in the room, and someone opened to call out a doctor.

"Dr. Moorehouse? She needs more oxygen—she's having trouble breathing!" The nurse shouted from the door to a doctor who was finalizing the wearing of the protective gear from the next room.

Dante's heart almost stopped. Machines were beeping in quick succession. He knew that sound all too well, and hope was thrown into the passing wind.

He was going to lose her.

And within five minutes his fears were confirmed.

Dante watched in horror as each nurse and doctor came out one by one with their heads down.

"Dr. Russo?" Dr. Moorehouse asked quietly.

Dante shook his head in disbelief.

"We're sorry for your loss, we did everything we could to save her," Dr. Moorehouse pronounced, watching Dante's legs buckle underneath him.

The news had hit him harder than a bombed wall. He was caught before he hit the ground and immediately put on medication and close monitoring. Samples of blood were taken to the lab as a precaution just to ensure that he didn't contract the disease from his wife. The hospital was a beehive of activity as news of Beth's death travelled faster than a forest fire.

All medical staff were given protective gear and the hospital hall looked like a preparation for a journey to the moon.

An hour later Dante woke up in an unfamiliar environment. He looked around trying to decipher where he was, and a few minutes later he finally recalled. He quickly rushed to the room where he had last seen his wife, almost knocking over some people who stood in his way. The room was eery and dark—it was locked from the inside. There were people inside fumigating the room. It was now clear that his wife had contracted the virus, and had died from it. He did not need rocket science to know this. Tears fell from his eyes as he cried his heart out.

He could not believe it!

Only this morning they were excitedly taking Skylar to school and driving together to work and … now?

Now?

Beth was *gone* … just like that?

What will he tell his daughter when he gets home?

FIVE

MASTERS ORTHOPEDIC MEDICAL CENTRE

DANTE SLOWLY FOUND his way back to the office, not talking to anyone on his way in. People stared at him with pitiful eyes. They had known Dante and Beth to be the happiest and healthiest people, and now seeing Dante in such sorrow was so heart breaking.

What did he need at the office that he had to go back there? In all his haste, he had forgotten his briefcase, wallet, cell phone … and Beth's purse, and shoulder bag.

He closed the door and locked himself inside. Word had already spread that tragedy had befallen the Russo's thus no one went knocking to disturb him. He knelt on the floor and sobbed painfully and silently. He felt so hopeless and helpless. For a moment he just wanted to die too. But then he remembered *Skylar.*

Sky needed her father now more than ever. Speaking of her, it was about time she was to be picked up from school. He was supposed to do this on his own now that his wife was … what?

Oh God! How was he going to do this?

He quickly reached for his cellphone and rung the house. Marni picked up the call on the third ring. He asked her to pick up Skylar from school using their other car since he had been held up at work. His voice was hoarse from crying, and Marni could feel that something was terribly wrong. However, she just responded without much asking and hurriedly went for the car key and drove off to school.

Just then Dante's buzzer went off on his office phone. A voice rang through the intercom:

"Dr. Russo?"

Dante wiped away his tears. "Yes?"

"Dr. Russo, the clinic administrator would like to speak to you before you leave."

Dante cleared his throat, "Yeah, sure."

On reaching the administrator's office, he was offered a seat and a glass of water.

James Henley, the clinic's administrator had known the doctors since the inception of the center. Beth and Dante had been inseparable since he had known them. They had always worked together in their department and they had earned the respect of all other fraternity. They were tightly knit. Looking at Dante right now, he saw a man full of sorrow and sadness, a man whose world had just fallen apart. He wished he could help him but there was nothing he could do. "I am truly sorry for your loss."

Dante's eye lids were still very heavy—he just wanted to go home. "Thank you."

"The staff are all in shock—after our meeting, I would like you to take a few weeks off."

"Thanks James, I appreciate it," Dante replied, waiting to be told why exactly he was there. He knew the administrator was stalling him for something else, and he was anxious to learn about it.

James cleared his throat. The government was pinning down on every case of Covid-19. He could not risk his job since this is where he earned his livelihood. This is where he got his kids school fees and his house rent. He had to choose his words wisely so that it would make his pain feel less painful. "I'm sure you're wondering why I called you here," he began, as Dante's eyes lit up ready to listen. "It's Beth, you know by now, she tested positive for the coronavirus —I've been informed that she was the very first case of Covid in this hospital, and since we know that she interacts with so many people in the clinic, we are afraid she may have infected others." James paused to look for some kind of reaction from Dr. Russo. There was none, he was still frozen in grief. He cleared his throat again. "Her body has been placed in an isolated morgue and as the government requires, she is supposed to be buried no later than seventy-two hours from the time of her death," he broke off with the most difficult news.

Dante reacted unexpectedly and jumped up in shock, "What! Seventy-two hours? I haven't even accepted that she's gone, and you're issuing me with a timer to mourn?"

Dante had never taken time to think about the people who had lost their loved ones and how they would react to such news. It had never affected him until now that he was walking in their shoes. He was certainly not prepared for this.

"I am so sorry, Dr. Russo, we're dealing with the government now, and as we speak, they are already aware that we lost a victim here today," James relayed, shifting in his chair.

Dante lowered his head in torment, "This is not happening. Can I see her at least?"

James swallowed hard. "No one is allowed to view her body since it's believed the virus is still very active in her blood, and it can be spread from one person to another."

"They can't do this! Do you know that apart from us, she has her family? A mother and father who adore her? They live in Canada for crissakes! And they still don't know—"

James shook his head and agreed with him. "Would you like me to contact them?"

Dante stared at the man contemplating it. "No—no, I'll do it. I'll tell them."

SIX

THREE MONTHS LATER

DANTE COULDN'T SLEEP.

The clinic had given him time to mourn—and mourn he did.

Self-pity soon morphed into guilt. A guilty conscious for not trying harder to be understanding towards his wife's feelings. Remorse for being a haughty husband. Truth be known, he had even thought about divorce. He knew deep down in his heart that they were not compatible—they had wanted different things, grew apart. Right after Skylar was born, he knew he wanted out of his marriage.

MARNI HILL always wanted to be a doctor, a pediatrician in fact, and even enrolled into medical school after graduation. But when Marni's father was killed in a car accident, Marni was left responsible to help provide for her younger siblings, ages sixteen and ten. Now her mother could stay home comfortably, while Marni's high paying nanny job afforded the foursome to keep their home and their lifestyle in tact.

Marni always loved children. That's why she chose wanting to study pediatric medicine. She wanted to help kids and to make sure they received the best possible care. So when she finally settled on becoming a nanny, nothing thrilled her more than knowing she could still lend a hand to a little human.

After Marni was vetted, she was hired by one of the most prestigious care facilities in the United States. ***"Helping Hand"*** was a premier domestic staffing and nanny placement agency serving the Los Angeles, New York City and San Francisco areas, as well as select locations around the world. They placed nannies, chefs, housekeepers, estate managers, and newborn care specialists with the utmost care and concern.

Marni was initially hired by the Russo's as a newborn care specialist, or "NCS" for short. A newborn care specialist was a non-medically trained newborn expert. A baby nurse (or NCS) would focus mainly on the infant, so the parents could rest. Marni would work overnight in a 12 or 24 hour shift and her duties would include:

• feeding

• bathing

• washing, cleaning & sterilizing bottles and other items related to the infant

• establishing sleep & feeding schedules

• swaddling, breastfeeding, umbilical cord & circumcision care consultation

• preparing the home for baby

The doctor's Russo both worked long hours, so Marni usually watched Skylar full-time. Marni was a "live-in" nanny, with her own room, bathroom and board. She stayed downstairs in the guest room with the baby while the Russo's lived upstairs. When Skylar was old enough to have her own room, Marni remained downstairs, while Skylar took the room across from her parents.

Marni loved her job—life was good until the day she realized she had fallen in love with her boss.

Dr. Dante Russo had come downstairs with just a towel around his waist, dripping wet from the hot shower he had taken to grab himself some extra shavers that were kept in a closet on the ground floor. He had thought he would go unseen, but to his surprise, Marni had just been in the kitchen making herself a sandwich while the doctors were upstairs getting ready for work.

In one moment, the universe had altered. Marni nearly dropped the mayo, Dr. Russo was so *hot*. *Gorgeous* was the word for him, with his chiseled abs, sun-tanned skin with a tuft of dark hair that led down to his lower regions. And his hair? All tasseled and wet, uncombed, slick like some GQ model on the cover of a magazine. As he walked away, she watched as his defined legs made their way back up the stairs, and in that minute she knew she would be ruined from crushing over that man.

She knew it was unrequited, as she practically died inside every time he would enter the nursery to gush over his little girl when he got home from work. A heavenly smile towards Marni would carry her through most nights—but then most nights were pretty lonely—and she ached for the morning when she could see him briefly again.

And yes, she did get a front row seat to the heated arguments that her employers would undergo. Grabbing Skylar's hand and leading her outdoors, away from the yelling and screaming. Disputes so heated, she sometimes wondered why they were even together, and scratched her head when they scheduled a vacation away.

And she loved that little girl like she was her own. Teaching her things, watching her mind expand and grow—it's all she ever wanted. Until …

Dr. Beth Russo passed away.

Now Dr. Russo barely makes it through the door sober. Drinking away his sorrows, or was it something else?

SEVEN

ONE-NIGHT HALF-DRUNK, Dante stumbled through the door. Marni had already tucked Skylar to bed and was awaiting his return so that she could serve his food before going to bed.

Yes, she made sure he ate, on most nights he wouldn't and would go straight upstairs to pass out without eating.

She had seen how much Dante was struggling and her heart went out to him.

"Dr. Russo," Marni barked at him before he stepped one foot on the staircase.

Dante peeked around the corner, "Yes?"

Marni nodded towards the small buffet of food she had spread across their large island. "I made some food, I think you should eat."

Dante eyed the exhibit of food across the quartz. "Okay, if you insist."

Marni smiled as he slowly walked towards her outstretched arms for him to take a seat on one of the bar stools.

Dante sat down and mistakenly smiled at her.

Marni nearly melted—whether intentional or non-intentional—his grin was so sensual, her heart could not stop racing.

Dante sat down, but didn't eat, instead he just stared at the food. "Everything looks delicious Marni, you've really outdone yourself."

Marni snickered, "This was unplanned—I just wanted to make sure you ate something today."

"I eat," Dante nodded, grabbing his fork and attempting to stab at a piece of roast meat.

Marni smiled inwardly, he was acting so cute, she simply had to calm her heart down. "Here, Dr. Russo …"

Dante nodded his head awkwardly, "Call me Dante —I insist you call me Dante now."

Marni gave him half a grin, "Okay, Dante, now eat."

Dante stabbed at the meat again, but missed it completely. Marni saw that he was struggling, so she took the fork away from his hand and scooped up a spoonful and spoon-fed him.

For a moment there Dante's drunkenness seemed to have disappeared, replaced by embarrassment. He thought about the gesture. In Marni, he saw a caring and loving, beautiful woman, something he had never noticed before when his wife was still alive. On the other hand, Marni saw a broken man, a man who felt so lost in the world of loneliness, a grieving man, a man who yearned for love and attention. She saw *vulnerability*.

In that moment, silent but connected emotions were exchanged by the way the spoon would scoop the food from the plate and entered a mouth. Before they knew it, they burned with eagerness—the spoon and food were forgotten—as lips crushed into each other with thirst that needed a different kind of water to quench the urge. There was hunger that desired a different kind of food. The fact that the feeling was mutual gave them comfortability.

Until Marni broke the kiss, and quickly collected the utensils and took them to the kitchen, fanning herself and trying to calm herself down.

Dante was left gasping for breath after the intense kissing. He just sat there in wonder and shock at what just happened—he felt so alive, and sexual attraction surged through him. He wondered if Marni had felt the same?

Marni was also having trouble washing the utensils. She had dropped three spoons in a span of one minute due to her hands shaking. She felt so guilty in that second, like she was taking advantage of the absence of Beth to kiss her husband.

She finished cleaning the utensils and was ready to go to bed. She was glad when she found that her boss had already gone to his. She turned off the lights and went to check on Skylar one more time before finally heading to her bedroom.

She changed into her pajamas, and leapt onto the bed and covered herself. On a normal day she would fall asleep immediately. But today she couldn't catch any sleep. She kept tossing and turning on the mattress. It was hot yet cold at the same time. She decided to take a cold shower maybe she would feel better afterwards, and actually get some good sleep. She stripped off her pajamas, and headed to the bathroom and had the shower. *What the heck was happening?!*

IN HIS ROOM, Dante was feeling overwhelmed by impulse, a need. He had never desired any other woman apart from his wife but now everything he had known was being put to the test, and he was failing terribly.

Damn his guilt …

Damn that magical kiss.

He could still feel it in his lips when he touched them. It was three months since his wife died and here, he was, already desiring and thinking about another woman? Something he never imagined would ever happen. But that kiss felt *so* good. "Better than Beth's," he muttered out loud. Now he was even comparing the two? He wondered if it had been real or he was just imagining things, but then Marni had kissed him back with the same intensity, same need, same burning desire. *What the heck was happening?!*

DANTE WAS NOW FULLY SOBER. The kiss the other day had drained the alcohol away somehow. All he could feel now was just a yearning that was pushing him to a nerve-racking edge. He was scared yet excited at the same time. He wanted *more* of it. He however didn't know how Marni would take it. With his arm bent under his head and on top of his pillow, he laid there in his bed looking at the ceiling. He didn't know what else to do to take that feeling away. A few minutes later he heard Marni's footsteps edging away as she went downstairs after putting Skylar to bed. Fresh desires rushed through him. He struggled hard to control them but they were so overwhelming, he felt himself getting rigid like when he was a teen.

Hopping out of bed he stripped off his boxers. *Maybe a cold shower would help?* He headed straight to the shower and let the cold water hit his burning skin. Looking down at his erection, he tried easing it down with the palm of his hand, until the slippery soap around his flesh only intensified the ache. He hadn't masturbated in years, but the feeling felt *so* satisfying. With every stroke, he thought of Marni. Kissing her lips, her neck, down to her naked breasts. Her nipples … pliable, *sexual … Oh God!* As the rise and fall of his hand swiftly increased over his hardness until he ejaculated all over the shower base. He was definitely beyond redemption. He was a goner.

THE NEXT NIGHT he contemplated on whether or not he should masturbate again in the cold shower. With his elbow bent under his head and on top of his pillow, Dante stared up at the ceiling.

He had to do this—face his fears. He had to face this or else he would be forever doomed to masturbating in the shower!

He threw off his duvets and went to face his fears. He didn't even knock at the door, he just pushed it open

—which coincidentally, Marni had been exiting the bathroom from just taking her own shower.

With only a loose towel wrapped around her body, she jumped in fear from the unexpected intrusion. When Marni saw who it was, she froze forgetting that she had just dropped the towel to the ground, and she was standing there naked.

She watched him in awe as his eyes trailed down the length of her. She wasn't embarrassed, on the contrary, the heat from his eyes alone were causing her blood to boil.

With the door closed and only a short distance to cover, Dante made a step towards Marni who was by now discovering what had taken place and with her feeble attempt at covering up her nudity, she grabbed the towel off the floor and shielded her torso.

"Can I help you with something?" She timidly managed to ask.

Dante gazed down at the ground, "I can't sleep."

Marni knew *why* he was in her room. She even had a notion of why he couldn't sleep. She had been wishing and hoping he'd close her bedroom door one day with him still on the inside.

They awkwardly stood there for some time, Marni waiting for Dante to explain what he wanted, and Marni to confess her longing for him.

Sighing heavily, Dante turned towards the door thinking of how bad an idea it was to have been in her room in the first place. Having second thoughts, he realized they had already broken a rule and there was no going back to their normal life again, especially after their kiss.

At his back, he heard, "Dr. Russo?"

"Dante," he corrected her. "Call me Dante."

Marni's carnal thoughts were driving her crazy! But she had to know—she had to know if he felt the same as she did. "Dante—"

"You know why I'm here right? I can't sleep because that kiss the other night is making me *unhinged*." He struggled to put the feeling into words so that Marni could somehow understand.

But Marni just looked at him and secretly smiled— she *did* understand—and dropped the towel on purpose, and walked backwards and laid seductively on her bed.

She watched in worship as Dante discarded himself of his boxers and walked over and laid down beside her. Warm, needy and vulnerable.

Kissing her neck first, she scooted underneath his long, muscular body and wrapped her arms around him, digging her fingers on his back drawing erotic circles. His lips were sensational, heavenly as she felt the better part of him grow and swell by the softness of her inner thigh. Opening up her legs for him to enter, she was surprised when he didn't, and expertly tried to finish her in other ways. Throwing her head back in delight, she felt his hand cup her breast and his hot wet kisses bear down around her nipple. Sucking, licking, biting her gently as his other hand inched its way toward the crux of her legs and a finger entered her wetness. Grabbing his head she bent in and locked her mouth with his, tongues dancing, erotic waltzing until her small whimpers of euphoria were too much for his ears.

"You're so beautiful," Dante huskily whispered.

At first Marni thought he had shoved his rock hard penis into her along with his fingers—the heaviness was so satisfying and welcomed—until she realized his hands were now around her backside, holding her passionately in an embrace. Huge and thick, he thrusted her seductively, till Marni could not hold in her orgasm any longer and mewled, *"Oh God!"*

Oh God indeed, as they tried to both calm their breathing, gradually descending from ecstasy, only to repeat their joy throughout the night.

NINE

DANTE SNAPPED out of his dream in the wee hours of the morning. His arms were wrapped tightly around a strange woman who was sleeping peacefully on his side. He looked around the almost unfamiliar room before everything came back to him. He had fallen asleep in her bed after having sex throughout the night. He felt a little bit *embarrassed* and a lot a bit *guilty*.

He slowly pulled his arms away from her body, and didn't even bother looking for his clothes. *Was he wearing clothes when he barged into her room last night?* He didn't remember, and hurriedly tip-toed towards her bedroom door. He especially did not want Skylar seeing him stark naked exiting her nanny's bedroom.

He closed the door gently behind him and gingerly half ran towards his bedroom and shut the door behind him. Leaning his head up against the back door he gazed around his unslept bed. The bed that he and Beth used to share. For some odd reason it felt like so long ago.

Shaking his head, trying to erase the unwanted memories, he headed towards his bathroom to wash off the night.

MARNI WOKE up later than usual. She had expected to see Dante lying next to her but she woke up to an empty bed. Nevertheless, the night before had been a busy one. She had loved every minute of it. His touches left her smiling as she closed her eyes and now, she was awake still smiling.

Oh God! 8:30 a.m., already?! Skylar had to be at school in thirty minutes! Marni rushed to the bathroom, took a quick rinse-off, got dressed and then woke Skylar up to get her dressed for school.

She was just about to head out Skylar's bedroom with the little girl's hand in hers when she bumped into Dante exiting his bedroom on his way into work. He was dressed nicely and he looked breathtaking before Marni's eyes cast down, embarrassed.

Dante had already concluded that he was going to let Marni dictate what happened between them. But he was privately disappointed when he noticed Marni uncomfortable in his presence.

"I'll take her to school today," he said, trying to cross out the awkwardness.

"Really daddy?" Skylar asked, running over to him and hugging his legs.

Dante leaned over and kissed her forehead, "Of course baby girl, there's nothing I'd love more."

Both adults were bashful and confused, while Skylar jumped down the stairs on their way towards the front door.

"Her breakfast?" Marni asked, as she grabbed Skylar's backpack off the hall tree.

Dante didn't look her in the eye, "We can grab something on the way."

"Donuts?" Skylar asked, placing her arms inside each shoulder strap of her backpack.

Dante laughed, "We'll see."

Five minutes later Marni watched father and daughter walk towards the car. *What a weird turn of events,* Marni thought, waving goodbye at the rear of the car as it drove away. She watched them turn the corner, and a small pang entered her heart. *He didn't even say good morning ...*

DANTE WAS glad for his five-year-old distraction, as Skylar seemed excited for a normal day to school. He drove toward the school chatting happily with his daughter who was happy that she was seated with him at the front of the car. On their way she didn't forget to point out the chance of donuts, or at least banana nut bread from Starbucks.

He dropped her off at school (after getting Starbucks, of course) and waved her goodbye promising that he would pick her up in the evening just like he used to.

Prekindergarten can be brutal.

His smile died down as he contemplated heading to work. *Did he really want to go to work today?* No. What he really wanted to do was to head back to his house and take Marni in his arms and make love to her again and again.

He turned his ignition on, but didn't pull out of the parking lot. *What was he gonna do?* Head to work as usual, turn on his computer, visit a few patients, eat lunch, then fumble through his computer again, see some more patients, then head back here to pick up Skylar?

Or …

TEN

DRIVING BACK HOME, he wondered what Marni would do. He replayed last night over and over in his head. It was mind blowing. He felt so young and alive! He felt so high—flying with the speed of a bullet. He didn't know if he should regret it, or be happy it happened. He picked the latter. It was hard to regret such a moment honestly, and he wasn't about to lie to himself anytime soon. The sheer feeling of being around her brought him pleasure.

Then, as he got closer to his neighborhood, Dante got cold feet. He decided that he was not going to broach the subject this soon. It was so unfair to Beth. Now he felt extremely guilty. He turned the car around, went back the opposite way, and sped off towards the main road.

Moments later he was kneeling with tears in his eyes. White roses in his hands. For the first time in the three months that his wife had passed he had decided to visit her grave in the cemetery. All he could do was shed painful tears as fresh memories came back to him in addition to his remorse. He felt so unworthy being there.

MARNI SAT in the living room and thumbed through a magazine she had bought at the market. Not really concentrating on one article in particular, she thought about Dante and their strange tension that morning. *Did he use her? Was she simply a convenience? A means to an end?* She had been in this position before—the ~~dreaded~~ surreal morning after. Bedded some stranger she met while clubbing one night, some random guy she didn't know, someone who wasn't worthy enough to get a last name.

Slapping the magazine shut, she threw her head back on the rim of the couch, and stared up at the ceiling. *But Dr. Russo, er, Dante was different*, she convinced herself. Loving her through the night, not once, but several times. Each and every time, better than before. He was a wonderful lover, and she wanted more! *She loved him,* she had concluded, *in love with him,* and she would wait until he came to her freely when he was ready…

UGH!

Or would she?

A small tear escaped the side of her eye and rolled down her cheek. Wiping it away, Marni brought her head straight and eyed a wedding photo he still had on their piano in the corner of the room. *Maybe he needs some time to think,* she thought again sadly. *Maybe I was just a diversion from his constant heartache? Maybe it was just his lack of self-control? Maybe I should just stop this pity party and get back to work?*

DANTE EVENTUALLY CALLED IN SICK, but didn't go home. As promised, he went to pick his daughter up from school.

As he drove, he realized he was getting nervous about going home. Apprehensive to go home? His own home? He hadn't felt this way since before Beth died. He was always stressed when he and Beth got home.

That is when the arguments would start. At work they played pretend, the happy couple, but the moment they stepped through their front door, there was no holds barred.

Skylar was so happy to see her father when she came out of class. He was early, and waited just outside with the other parents for five minutes and as soon as she saw him, she came running right into his open arms. Oh how he had missed such moments. The little girl hugged him tightly as if she understood her father's pain.

When he buckled her into her car seat, she had been wearing this beautiful smile that she had gotten from her mother. He was happy about that.

MARNI HAD BEEN WAITING by the door. As always, she was so happy to see Skylar who felt the same way. She immediately told her about school and how daddy bought her candy on their way home. The little girl was so chatty that Dante slipped by the two females and headed inside. As Marni took Skylar to the kitchen to have some real food, Dante went straight up the staircase, to escape temptations.

EPILOGUE

THE NEXT DAY

DANTE WOKE up early to prepare to go to work. He checked everything he needed to carry and when he was satisfied, he went straight to the kitchen intending on grabbing something quick for breakfast. To his surprise, he found Marni and Skylar already at the table. Marni was feeding Skylar and making sure she didn't mess up her school uniform.

"Good morning daddy!" Skylar greeted. "Nanny Marni woke me up urrlie to eat some eggs."

Dante glanced at his daughter's half-eaten breakfast, "Good morning baby. Did you sleep well?"

"Yes daddy, you hungry? Nanny Marni made some breakfast for you too."

In that moment, Dante raised his eyes towards Marni to catch her staring at him. She was waiting on his reply and when he gave none, he stepped over to the coffee pot and poured himself a cup.

He decided he was going to face his fears again and tried to solicit her attention, but Marni wouldn't look him straight in the eye. She concentrated on his daughter.

The silence between them felt deafening, a chokehold he simply had to loosen. Dante felt awful that he hadn't spoken to her until now. He decided he was not going to act like a coward anymore and decided to talk to Marni. He had to talk to her about *something* …as long as it was speech.

"I'm dropping Skylar off at school again," he said, sort of matter-of-factly. "If you need me, call me," he told her after not making eye contact with her again.

Marni just nodded. She knew it was just pure words. Inside, her heart was breaking. Its not like she had ever called him before. She was always well prepared. She sensed Dante's eyes on her and she turned to look at him too.

Their eyes lock and hold.

If not for Skylar to urge her dad to hurry so that they wouldn't be late, they would have continued with their staring contest.

Dante got into the car and drove off.

MARNI SLOWLY CLOSED the door and burst into tears. Why did it ache so much? Living with heartache was torment, seeing him everyday was suffering in itself. *Should I quit?* She couldn't quit, she had to keep paying the bills, keep a roof over her family's head. *Oh God, what should I do?*

DANTE SAT in the parking lot of the school contemplating his next move. Part of him wanted to drive back to his house and grab Marni in his arms, the other part mentioned that someday he needed to go back to work.

He chose the latter, and put his SUV in gear and headed downtown. He was just about to get off the freeway, when his heart began to thump. Something told him he was making a **huge** mistake...

MARNI SPOTTED their dog pawing the back door wanting to go outside. She stumbled over to the door and let the dog out, she then headed towards the kitchen and blew her nose on a paper towel. Eyeing the breakfast dishes, she decided to rinse them off and place them all into the dishwasher. One by one, she placed each dish into their own slot, rinsing and shaking each plate until the washer was full. She was just about to close the door when she spotted Dante filling the entryway.

Their eyes lock and hold.

Until Dante finally stepped forward, placed down his car keys and briefcase, and came into the kitchen.

Marni gradually closed the washer and then shyly looked down at the ground. Her heart was beating a mile a minute ... *did he come back for her?* "Dr. Russo?"

"Dante," he interrupted her again. "My name is Dante."

Marni bit down on her lower lip—Dante was so handsome with his shoulders and posture in an exposed stance.

He cleared his throat before saying, "I'm sorry we're only getting to talk now."

Marni shook her head, "I know, you've been busy."

Then silence again.

Dante stepped into her. "You've been with us for a long time now Marni, caring about my daughter as if she was your own. I feel so lucky that you were here."

Marni gulped. *These weren't words of love, these were words of a goodbye!* "Are you letting me go?"

Dante circled his eyes around her face, "Yes."

Marni closed her eyes—bit down on her lower lip—she was about to burst into tears again! She was just about to turn and walk away when Dante held her arm back.

"Where you going?"

Marni gazed deep into his eyes, "Upstairs, to pack."

Dante let go a small smile, "I wasn't finished."

Marni's heart began to calm down, she reacted instinctively to his magnetism and wit. "No?"

Dante's heart melted with the curve of her sweet smile, "No." He then pulled her closer to him and wrapped one arm around the small of her back. "I just thought it best that you weren't working here while we slept together. It would be wrong."

Marni's heart leapt for joy! "Sleep together?"

Dante leaned in and kissed the tip of her nose. "Yes, *sleep*—among other things," he confessed, brushing a hair away from her lovely face. He bore into her eyes, "I've developed strong feelings for you, I was afraid to face them, but I realized that life is too short."

Marni tilted her chin and gave him a small peck on his lips, "I have feelings for you too."

Dante now fully smiled and allowed the declaration to warm his body, overcome his fear. "If there's one thing that I learned about losing Beth, is that life is *too* short, and we should jump on the opportunities when we get them."

Marni closed the space between them and now fully embraced him, locking her arms around his backside. Feeling him clasp her body in return, she whispered, "I'll jump when you say jump."

Dante laid his cheek on the top of her head, "So I say, let's jump already."

The two inclined simultaneously and kissed, as a new kind of love was born.

THE END

ACKNOWLEDGMENTS

PlayStation

Maldives

California

Los Angeles

Cedars Sinai Medical Center

GQ Magazine

Starbucks

About Savannah

Savannah Kole is an author of Contemporary Romance and Modern Fiction. Savannah has many writing interests and lives an incognito digital lifestyle.

Savannah is part of the Ardent Artist Books family and is the author of several published books.

amazon.com/Ardent-Artist-Books/e/B08BX8F1DZ

youtube.com/theardentartist

Also by Savannah

◆ Single Dad Nanny Romance ◆

Forbidden Love

◆ Alpha Male Curvy Woman Romance ◆

The Butterfly

Pop Fly Kiss

Meet Me on Social Media